To Mum and Dad — P.M.
To Brittany — G.P.

MYRIAD BOOKS LIMITED
35 Bishopsthorpe Road, London SE26 4PA

First published in 1997 by
FRANCES LINCOLN LIMITED
4 Torriano Mews, Torriano Avenue, London NW5 2RZ

ISBN 1 84746 003 8

EAN 9 781 84746 003 5

Printed in China

ELEPHANTS
don't do
ballet

Penny McKinlay

Illustrated by Graham Percy

MYRIAD BOOKS LIMITED

One Christmas, Esmeralda was given a musical box with a tiny gold ballerina on top. When the music played, the ballerina twirled elegantly round on one leg.

"I want to be a ballerina," said Esmeralda.

Her brother Ernest snorted into his bucket of milk. "Elephants don't do ballet!"

"Now, Ernest," said Mummy.

Esmeralda tied a knot in her trunk. "I want to be a ballerina!"

Mummy sighed. "Yes, dear. I'll see about lessons."

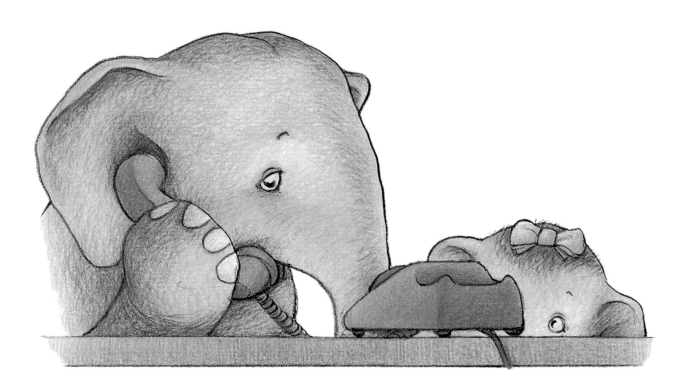

Next day, Mummy rang the ballet school.
"She'll need a leotard," said the ballet teacher.
"A pink one. And pink ballet shoes. Be here at six
o'clock sharp."

The man in the dance shop looked worried when
he saw Esmeralda. Mummy curled her trunk and
coughed delicately.

"Um, Large, would you say?"

But even Extra Extra Large didn't fit.

Esmeralda tied a knot in her trunk and stamped
her foot. The shop shook.

"I think we'd better go, dear," said Mummy.

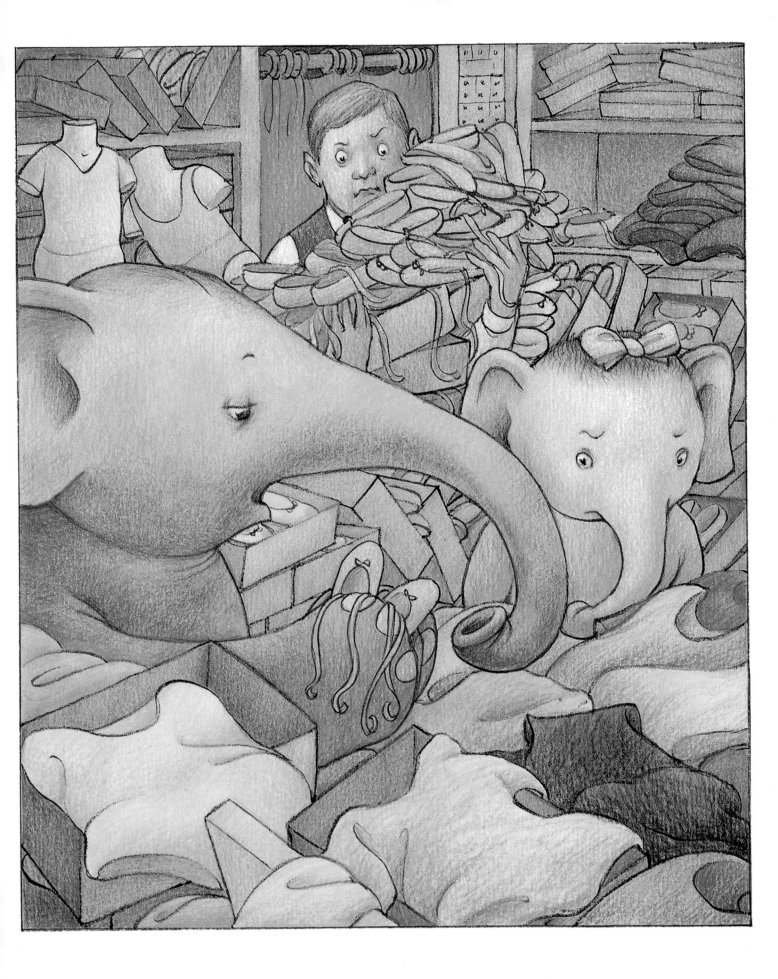

On the way home they passed a furniture store.
A sign in the window caught Mummy's eye.

MR MIRACLE'S CHAIR COVERS
STRETCH TO FIT THE LARGEST SEAT!

"Do you have those in pink?" enquired Mummy.

They did – and they fitted perfectly. Esmeralda did
a delighted twirl and the chandelier shook.
    They even had pink footstool covers to match.
    "We'll take four!" Mummy trumpeted in triumph.

Shortly before six they arrived at the ballet class.
Silence fell as Esmeralda trundled in.
Someone giggled. "She's fat!" said a small voice.

Esmeralda tied a knot in her trunk.

"Ignore them, Esmeralda," said Mummy. "And do untie your trunk, dear. It doesn't look nice."

The lesson started. Mummy wrapped her trunk tightly around her eyes and ears.

"First, girls," said the teacher, "we shall learn to point our toes. Right foot, clap, left foot, clap. Off we go!"

Esmeralda got in a terrible tangle. She pointed both right feet at once, and capsized.

The ballet teacher called out, "Try pointing your back feet and clapping with your front, Esmeralda. See you all next week, girls!"

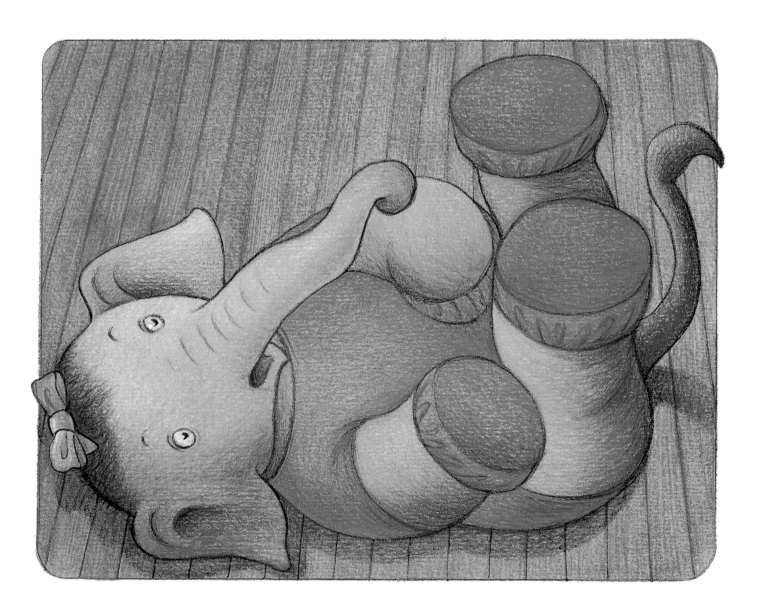

The next week, Mummy folded her ear-flaps over her eyes.

"Today, girls, we shall learn to trot like little ponies," said the ballet teacher.

The class trotted in a circle.

"Now, girls, we shall gallop!" cried the teacher.

There were muffled screams as Esmeralda lumbered into a gallop. The ballet teacher hauled the girls out from under Esmeralda's feet.

"In future, Esmeralda, stick to a trot," said the teacher. "See you next week, girls!"

The next week, Mummy wore ear-plugs and did a crossword.

"Today, girls, we shall learn to twirl," said the teacher.

But when Esmeralda twirled, her trunk wrapped itself so tightly round her neck, she couldn't breathe. By the time she got it untangled, her face was blue.

"Next time, Esmeralda, try holding a wand in your trunk," said the teacher. "See you next week, girls!"

The next week, Mummy wore headphones and did her knitting.

"Today, girls, we shall learn to jump!" said the teacher. "One at a time, I think," she added nervously, looking at Esmeralda.

Esmeralda soared up... and crashed down on to a loose plank. The ballerina on the other end flew up to the roof.

"Perhaps more of a skip, Esmeralda?" suggested the teacher, fetching a ladder. "Six o'clock next week, girls!"

The next week, Mummy turned her back and read the newspaper.

"This week, girls, we shall reach up and pick stars," said the ballet teacher.

Esmeralda stretched her stumpy little legs, up, up...
and tottered heavily back on to the grand piano.
    While they waited for an ambulance to take the
pianist away, the teacher said: "Try using your trunk
to pick stars, Esmeralda. Now remember, girls, next
week is our show!"

At last it was the night of the show.
The music began.
The curtain started to rise. And stopped.
It rose a little more. And stopped.
Esmeralda's two back feet were planted firmly on the bottom of the curtain.

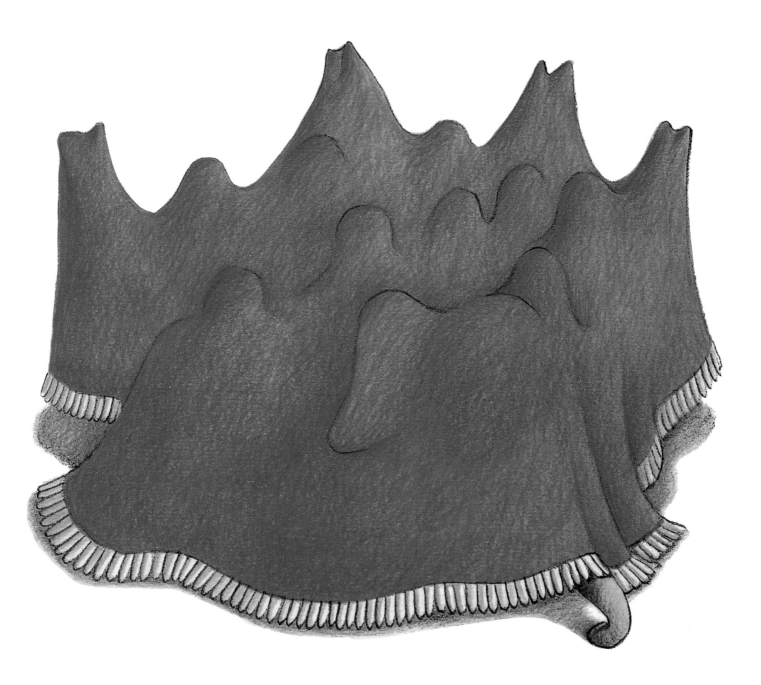

"Move your feet, Esmeralda!" hissed the teacher.
Too late. There was a loud rip – and the curtain
came crashing down, burying Esmeralda and all the
little ballerinas in an orange velvet heap.

Then a trunk emerged from under the curtain.
With a heave, Esmeralda rose and twirled the
curtain gracefully above her head, while the little
ballerinas clung to the edges like stars.

Esmeralda lowered the curtain and the ballerinas
danced around her as she stood with the orange
velvet curtain draped about her, like a queen.

In a grand finale, each little ballerina leaped lightly on to Esmeralda's trunk and pirouetted perfectly, like the little ballerina on the Christmas musical box.

Afterwards, the audience clapped as if they
would never stop.
"Well done, Esmeralda!" cried the ballet teacher.
Mummy hugged Esmeralda tightly with her trunk.
Ernest tugged Esmeralda's tail. "You were right,"
he said. "Elephants *can* do ballet."

On the way home, they passed the ice-skating
rink. Outside was a picture of a lady skating.
Esmeralda's eyes glinted.
"I want to be an ice-skater!" she said.
Ernest choked on his bubble gum.
"Elephants can't..."

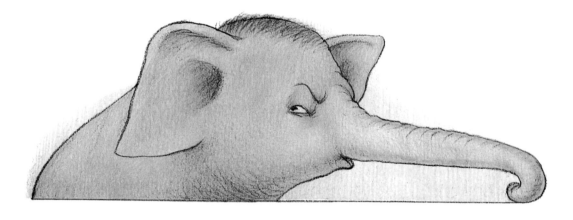

"I want to be an ice-skater!"
Esmeralda stamped. The pavement cracked.
Mummy sighed. "Yes, dear," she said.
"I'll see about lessons."